THE BANANA CABANA

Meet

HOWIE

the hotel manager.
Howie likes: trampolines,
running fast, ear wax.
Howie dislikes: silence,
quitters, bubble baths.

Meet

DUCK

the hotel's handy animal.
Duck likes: sand castles, lasers,
alternate universes.
Duck dislikes: bread crumbs,
cloudy days, itchy feet.

First published in Great Britain in 2013 by Hodder Children's Books

Written by Sarah Courtauld
Interior layout by ninataradesign.com

A Catalogue record for this book is available from the British Library.

ISBN: 978 1 444 91391 0

Printed in Spain

The paper and board used in this paperback by Hodder Children's Books are natural
recyclable products made from wood grown in sustainable forests. The manufacturing
processes conform to the environmental regulations of the country of origin.

Hodder Children's Books
A division of Hachette Children's Books
338 Euston Road, London NW1 3BH
An Hachette UK company
www.hachette.co.uk

shouted Howie.

The sun was shining, the sky was blue, and Howie was feeling pretty pleased with himself. He was grinning from ear to ear. He was leaping from paw to paw.

'Wait till you see this!' he said.

His friends weren't feeling quite so thrilled.

'We still don't know why you dragged us out here!' said Bunny, who was standing with the rest of Howie's friends, outside the Banana Cabana.

'Because I'm following in the footsteps of my gravity-defying, action-loving, all-time hero, Dirk Danger …'

So, who's Dirk Danger then?
Only the greatest stunt hero of all time!
You couldn't even count the number of rings of fire he's jumped through, cliffs he's jumped off, pants he's set fire to, or bumps on the head he's got.

'I'm going to attempt the triple, quadruple, tightrope, quasi-vertical flight of fear!' said Howie.
He climbed up on to the top of the huge, rickety wooden ramp outside the Banana Cabana.

Noooooooooooooooo

came a chorus from all his friends. They'd seen Howie attempt the triple, quadruple, tightrope, quasi-vertical flight of fear before. It never ended well.

'This time,' said Howie, 'unlike the other four hundred and fifty-seven times I tried, I'm going to land it FOR SURE!'

'Howie,' said his friend Octo, 'maybe you should just think a little, about ...' Howie jumped up on to his unicycle, and sped straight off the edge of the platform.

'Never mind,' Octo trailed off.

Howie flew down the wooden ramp ...

He whizzed up into the air ...

YAAAAAAAAA!!!

… He landed on the tightrope of impossibility, and wobbled and wiggled his way along it …

'What is he THINKING?' sighed Bunny, as she watched him go.

YEARGH! Howie had succeeded in wobbling all his way to the end of the tightrope of impossibility. Next, he dived on to the springboard of terror. He flew into the air, about to take on the next stage: the three-storey super-fast spiral slide …

Howie landed, face first, on the edge of the giant three-storey super-fast spiral slide. His face stuck to the edge of the slide for a moment ...

... before he fell, headfirst, towards the ground.

'Ta-da!' said Howie, when he'd pulled his head out of the earth.

Hmmmn, he thought ...

Howie's thoughts:
Eyes looking in different directions — check.
Stars floating around head — check.
Whole world gently swaying — check.
Full marks!

'OK!' Howie said brightly, only slightly slurring his words. 'Who's ready to see attempt number four hundred and fifty-nine?'

'Howie, don't!' said Octo, peeking out from behind his tentacles. Even thinking about his friend doing the stunt made him so worried he nearly inked himself.

But Howie was already getting ready for his next attempt.

'Come on! Watch me!' he said, running back to the start board. There was a whole constellation of stars above his head now, and that could only be a good thing.

CHAPTER 2

Over at the Chateau Chattoo, Poodle was jumping up and down with excitement. Her special delivery had just arrived, and when her winged sidekick Batty opened it up, Poodle shrieked with delight.

'Look at it — it's perfect,' she said. 'Well, considering the subject.'

'What's it for?' Batty asked, looking at the strange, shiny metal object. It had Howie's face. Howie's body. Howie's arms, and Howie's tail. It definitely reminded him of someone …

'Meet Robo-Howie,' Poodle said proudly. 'I'm going to trick all of Howie's little friends into thinking that this robot is really him. And when I have them in the palm of my hand, I'm going to drive them all away from the Banana Cabana.' Poodle cackled mischievously. 'Ha, ha, hee, hee, ha, ha.'

'Hee hee hee ha ha ha ha!' sniggered Batty.

'Quiet!' snapped Poodle. 'This is MY moment.'

'Sorry, boss,' said Batty.

'Now, let's test it out. Robot, speak ill of Howie!'

The robot's antenna flashed to life, and a strange, computerised voice said:

I am Howie. I. Am. A. Stinkhead.

Poodle clapped her hands with glee.
'Robot,' she said,
'kick Howie in the butt.'
A door at the back of Robo-Howie opened, a large brown boot swung out, and the robot kicked itself in the butt.
'This is going to be fantastic!' said Poodle. 'Once I drive all of Howie's friends from the Banana Cabana, he'll be lost! He'll never be able to run it on his own. He'll be forced to give the entire hotel to me. Me! Me! Me!'
She laughed.
Robo-Howie laughed.
Batty remembered not to laugh.

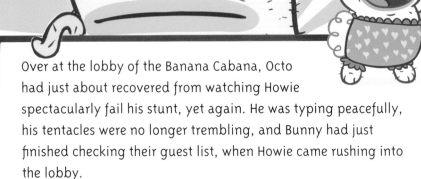

Over at the lobby of the Banana Cabana, Octo
had just about recovered from watching Howie
spectacularly fail his stunt, yet again. He was typing peacefully,
his tentacles were no longer trembling, and Bunny had just
finished checking their guest list, when Howie came rushing into
the lobby.

'Howie, what are you doing?' asked Octo.

Howie was dressed in some strange red padding. He looked like
a cross between a ladybird and a centipede.

'I'm re-attempting the triple, quadruple, tightrope, quasi-vertical flight of fear!'

'Oh no!' said Octo and Bunny. 'Not again!'

'Come on, who's watching?' said Howie, and he bounded away.

Barely a moment later, Octo and Bunny turned to see … what they *thought* was Howie, back in the lobby.

Only this 'Howie' had just come in from the door opposite the one Howie had just run out of.

'Hello. Banana Cabana employees,' came a weirdly mechanical voice.

'Howie?' asked Octo. 'How did you get around to the other side of the hotel?'

'Hello. Banana Cabana employees,' the voice repeated.

'And why are you talking so strangely?' said Octo.

'Hello, Banana Cabana employees,' said Duck, in a weirdly mechanical voice. He'd just turned up, wearing a colander helmet.

Hmmmn, thought Octo. *Howie is being a little weird. But compared to Duck, he's … pretty normal.*

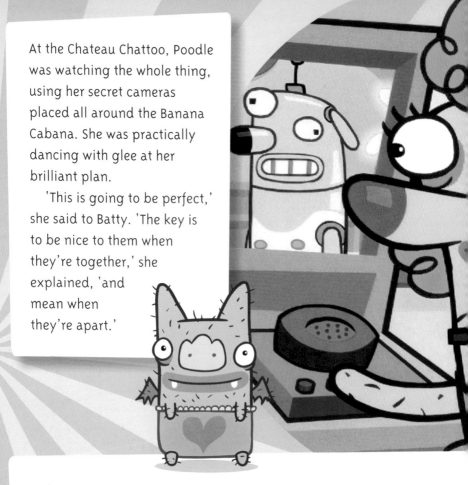

At the Chateau Chattoo, Poodle was watching the whole thing, using her secret cameras placed all around the Banana Cabana. She was practically dancing with glee at her brilliant plan.

'This is going to be perfect,' she said to Batty. 'The key is to be nice to them when they're together,' she explained, 'and mean when they're apart.'

'Robot,' she said. 'Compliment Octo and Bunny!'

The robot looked across the desk at Octo. 'You look very nice today,' Robo-Howie said. 'Octopus. You are looking very muscular. You must have been. Working. Out.'

'Gee,' said Octo, 'I didn't think anyone was going to notice!' His tentacle curls must really have paid off.

The robot turned to Bunny.

'Rabbit,' it said, 'you in no way look weird. Or gross today.'

'Thanks, Howie!' said Bunny. She'd spent about four hours getting ready this morning, and she was glad it was time well spent.

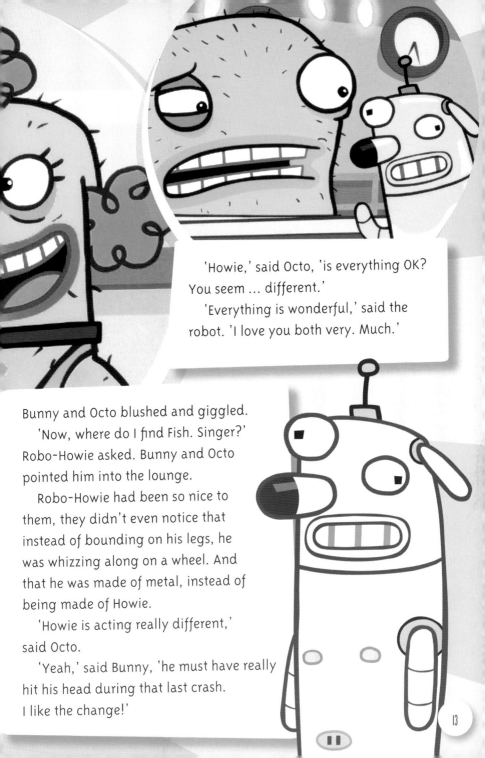

'Howie,' said Octo, 'is everything OK? You seem ... different.'

'Everything is wonderful,' said the robot. 'I love you both very. Much.'

Bunny and Octo blushed and giggled.

'Now, where do I find Fish. Singer?' Robo-Howie asked. Bunny and Octo pointed him into the lounge.

Robo-Howie had been so nice to them, they didn't even notice that instead of bounding on his legs, he was whizzing along on a wheel. And that he was made of metal, instead of being made of Howie.

'Howie is acting really different,' said Octo.

'Yeah,' said Bunny, 'he must have really hit his head during that last crash. I like the change!'

13

In a cloud of smoke, Howie had arrived.

'Howie?' said Octo.

'You guys should have seen that!' Howie gasped. 'I was so close to landing it this time! Good thing I came out of it unharmed,' he added, as a huge jet of flame burst out of his pants and set off the fire alarm, and the sprinkler, just about dousing the flames.

'Hmmm,' said Howie. 'Do you smell something?'

While Howie's pants smouldered gently, back at the Chateau Chattoo Poodle was ready to deploy the next stage of Operation Robo-Howie in the lounge.

Narwhal, the Banana Cabana's one and only celebrity entertainer and whale, was rehearsing for his evening show.

(If by rehearsing, you mean: *reading an article about himself in Narwhal Weekly, and thinking: 'Hey baby, I'm pretty great. No one's quite as great as me. Look at the shine on that horn.'*)

'Singer,' said Robo-Howie, whizzing into the lounge, 'your singing is. No. Good. Singing is easy. Anyone can sing.'

Robo-Howie got out a microphone to prove it. 'Singy sing, sing sing,' he sang, tunelessly.

Narwhal flapped his fins in rage.

'You really think you can do what I do?' said Narwhal. 'I do fifteen minutes a show, three nights a week, two weeks a month, four months a year, three years out of FIVE!'

He jabbed his fin at Robo-Howie.

'I wrote, directed and performed a one-whale play! I look fantastic in bonnets, baby! I can hold lollipops — not only tiny ones, but medium-size ones! You really think you could do all of THAT?'

'Yes,' said Robo-Howie.

WELL GOOD LUCK, BABY, COS I QUIT!

Narwhal flounced out of the lounge. He was a whale of talent, and he wasn't going to waste it on the Cabana any longer. There were bound to be other hotels out there. Other hotels where his singing would be loved. Where audiences would laugh, would weep, would give him standing ovations.

The world was waiting. Waiting for a whale with a dream.

Meanwhile, Howie was strolling through the lobby, when he ran into an extremely handsome stranger.

'Looking good, my friend,' he said.

'Um ... ditto,' said Robo-Howie.

'You look kind of familiar,' said Howie.

'Huhhhh ...' said Robo-Howie.

'It's just something about you,' said Howie. 'You remind me of somebody ...'

'No. I. Don't,' said Robo-Howie.

'OK!' said Howie with a shrug, and they went their separate ways ...

In the kitchen, Piggy was cooking delicious pancakes. Piggy was a master of pancakes. They were buttery, sugary and lemony. With a few other secret ingredients.

'Hello, Pig,' said Robo-Howie, whirring up behind Piggy just as he was mid-flip.

'Dog thing,' said Piggy.

'Pig, you are fired,' said Robo-Howie.

Piggy dropped his frying pan.

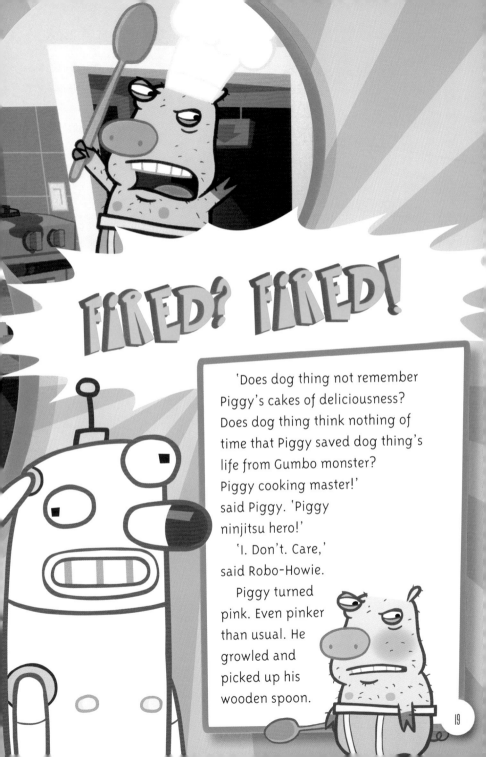

FIRED? FIRED!

'Does dog thing not remember Piggy's cakes of deliciousness? Does dog thing think nothing of time that Piggy saved dog thing's life from Gumbo monster? Piggy cooking master!' said Piggy. 'Piggy ninjitsu hero!'

'I. Don't. Care,' said Robo-Howie.

Piggy turned pink. Even pinker than usual. He growled and picked up his wooden spoon.

19

'Dog thing, I SCOOP YOU!!' Piggy yelled. He ran at Robo-Howie, preparing for a ninjitsu move of incredible power. Just as he was about to hit him, hard, something strange happened.

Howie's arms started whizzing around. They deflected the scoop. Howie was completely unscathed.

And he didn't yell, or run away ...

'Something different with dog thing,' Piggy muttered, scratching his chin, and picking up his scoop.

Dog thing stand tall. Dog thing not feel pain. Dog thing have power. Piggy respect Howie's wishes. Piggy pack and humbly go.

Soon, Piggy was ready to go. He'd packed all his things.

Inside Piggy's suitcase:
White hatty things
Scoopy thing
Emergency pancakey thing
Reserve emergency pancakey thing
One more emergency pancakey
thing for journey

On his way out of the Banana Cabana, Piggy ran into Narwhal, who had also packed all his most precious possessions.

Inside Narwhal's suitcase:
Horn wax
Framed pictures of Narwhal
The Complete Works of Narwhal
Narwhal's greatest hits
Narwhal's autobiography: *Being Narwhal*
Narwhal's screenplays:
When Narwhal Met Narwhal
Four Narwhals and a Narwhal and
Narwhal: Prince of Whales

They were both leaving the Banana Cabana, never to return. Just as they reached the door, they ran into none other than the villain who had just fired them — Howie.

'There he is,' said Narwhal angrily. 'You're a real sour note, you know that?'

'Thanks, Narwhal!' said Howie, brightly.

'Why, you smug little ...'

Narwhal threw himself at Howie, fins first. Piggy (who knew all about Howie's new, ninjitsu powers) had to use all his strength to pull Narwhal off Howie.

'Feel the power of my horn!' Narwhal roared, waving his horn pointlessly in the air.

'Narwhal, what *are* you doing?' asked Octo, who was watching the scene, completely confused.

'What am I doing? What am I DOING?!' said Narwhal. 'Your little fleabag of a friend fired Piggy. And when I threatened to quit, like I do every day, instead of insisting that I stay — like he does every day — he just let me walk right out the door!'

'That's weird,' said Howie. 'I don't remember firing Piggy.'

At this, Narwhal burst into tears. Weeping was one of his many talents, and it seemed too good an opportunity to miss. 'Does your evil know no bounds, baby?' he asked Howie.

CHAPTER 3

Of course, Poodle wasn't satisfied with just sacking Piggy and Narwhal. She wanted to get rid of all Howie's friends. And so Robo-Howie was already on his next mission ... to Duck's shed.

Things you should know about Duck's shed:
Nothing.
Just don't ask.
Really, it's better that you don't know.

'Hello, handy-animal whose name escapes me, you are fired!' said Robo-Howie, finding Duck outside his shed. (Really, it was lucky that he didn't have to go inside. Trust me.)

Duck glanced up at his strange visitor. It looked like Howie, but ...

'Something is weird,' said Duck, pulling his magnifying glass out of his pants, and peering right at him.

'Incorrect,' said Robo-Howie. 'Nothing is weird.'

'Oh,' said Duck. 'You have a speck of dirt on your nose. I will get it!'

And he picked up his handy hose, and sprayed Robo-Howie in the face.

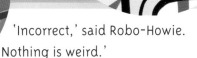

SPLOOOOOOSHAAAA!!!

As some unhappy robots know — particularly those who have taken beach holidays — electricity and water are not good friends. Really, they should never meet. As the jet of water gushed inside Robo-Howie, and soaked his wires, the robot ...

Fizzed.

It whizzed to the
left. And to the right.
It spluttered. Bright
yellow sparks flew out
of it.

Finally, it leaned over to one side, muttered 'turnip', and sighed a terrible sigh.

'Agreed,' said Duck.

'I can't believe that piece of junk broke down already!' Poodle fumed. She had seen the whole scene on her secret cameras. Now she was watching as clouds of purple smoke billowed out of the broken robot.

'It really is just like Howie,' she sighed. 'Batty, fix that robot immediately!'

'But Poodle, I don't know how—'

'Fix it now, before it attracts attention!' Poodle screamed.

'Uh … OK, boss,' said Batty, glumly.

'Great! Now, step just a little to your left,' said Poodle sweetly. 'That's right.'

'Um, sure,' said Batty. 'But I don't get it. Why do you want me to ...'

'Perfect!' said Poodle. And at the touch of a remote control, a springboard opened up in the floor just under Batty's feet.

And sent him ...

FLYING!

Oh. I get it now.

Poodle's aim must have been pretty good, because Batty landed just next to the broken robot.

'Hello, Duck,' said Batty cheerfully. 'Don't mind me.'

He opened up the back of the robot, and started fiddling with the wires.

YARHHHHHH!!!

Batty yelled, as a massive jolt of electricity shot through him.

A second jolt knocked him off his feet and set his pants on fire.

Luckily, Duck still had his hose at the ready. He doused Batty in a jet of water.

'YARGHHHHH!!' screamed Batty, who was now being thoroughly electrocuted.

'My work here is done,' said Duck, and he waddled away.

Batty waited until he stopped fizzing, and then he opened up the robot's door, and looked at the tangle of wires inside. They were crackling and sparking.

'Batty!' came Poodle's voice.

Batty had almost forgotten that he'd packed his walkie-talkie.

'Batty, fix that robot immediately, before someone notices!'

'Uh … OK, I'm uh, going in,' he said to Poodle.

'Just fix it!' Poodle screeched back.

With a groan, Batty forced himself through the door. 'Why didn't I listen to my parents and stay in clown college?' he muttered.

He was now inside the robot. Lots of wires were sparking and fizzing around him. But there were lots of levers too.

Hmmmn, thought Batty. He had an idea …

CHAPTER 4

'I still don't understand why I would have tried to kick you guys out of the hotel!' said Howie, who was surrounded by all his friends, staring at him sadly.

'You're sure your brain wasn't damaged when you crashed?' said Bunny.

'Not any more than usual, peanut butter,' said Howie, his eyes going glassy, just for a moment.

'Piggy stumped,' said Piggy. 'Piggy want to stay at hotel, but Piggy like Howie much more than dog thing.'

'Thanks, Piggy,' said Howie. It was the first nice thing that anyone had said to him all day.

'Not you, dog thing,' said Piggy. 'Piggy talk about Howie!'

'I'm Howie!' said Howie.

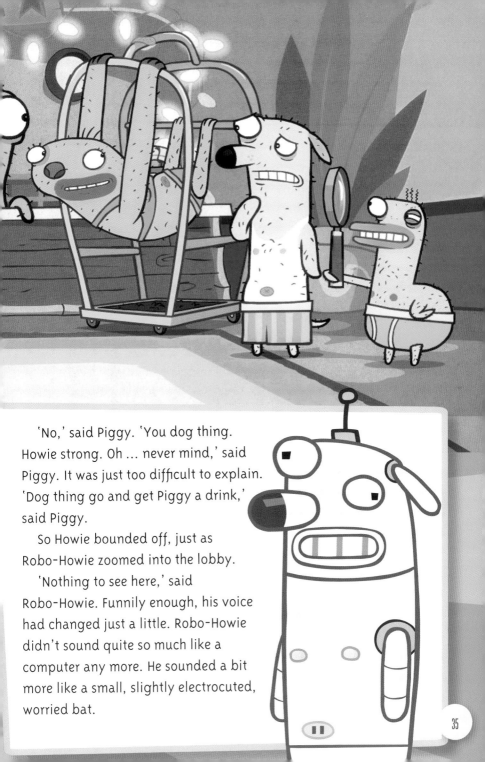

'No,' said Piggy. 'You dog thing.
Howie strong. Oh ... never mind,' said
Piggy. It was just too difficult to explain.
'Dog thing go and get Piggy a drink,'
said Piggy.

So Howie bounded off, just as
Robo-Howie zoomed into the lobby.

'Nothing to see here,' said
Robo-Howie. Funnily enough, his voice
had changed just a little. Robo-Howie
didn't sound quite so much like a
computer any more. He sounded a bit
more like a small, slightly electrocuted,
worried bat.

'Just a normal, non-robotic dog going about its business,' Robo-Howie said.

'Robot,' Poodle hissed down the walkie-talkie. 'Forget the original plan. Fire everyone!'

'You are all fired!' said the robot.

Howie's friends stared at him in shock. It just didn't make any sense.

'Even me?' said Octo.

'Yes, you too. Kelp breath,' said Robo-Howie.

'But Howie, I'm your best friend!' said Octo.

'Friend end,' said Robo-Howie.

'Don't you remember how … we went on so many adventures together? Don't you remember how I even re-named happiness Howieness, just for you! How you cured me of my fear of heights? How we took part in Dirk Danger's stunt movie — together!'

'No,' said Robo-Howie. 'No, no, no, no.'

'Robot,' Poodle hissed down the walkie-talkie. 'Stop wasting time. Just get rid of them!'

'You are all fired,' Robo-Howie said again.

That bump on the head really did change Howie, Octo thought sadly. It was no use. And with the other animals, he shuffled miserably out of the lobby, just as …

... the real Howie bounded back in, holding a drink for Piggy.

'Hey — whoah — where is everyone?' asked Howie. But there was no one there apart from the handsome guest he'd met earlier.

'So, how is it? Enjoying your stay? Like the hotel? There is something familiar about you,' Howie said, with a smile.

'No there isn't,' said Robo-Howie.

'You're so handsome,' said Howie. 'I definitely feel like we've met before.'

'I don't think so,' said Robo-Howie, nervously.

'You definitely remind me of someone. Wait. Did you go to Camp Lake Boogerwater?' said Howie.

No response from Robo-Howie.

Howie was still chatting away to his new, handsome friend, when the others came back into the lobby. Now they had all packed their bags, ready to leave the Banana Cabana forever. They looked utterly miserable ... and then, as they saw Howie and his new friend, they all looked ... confused.

'What's going on?' said Bunny, looking from one Howie to the other.

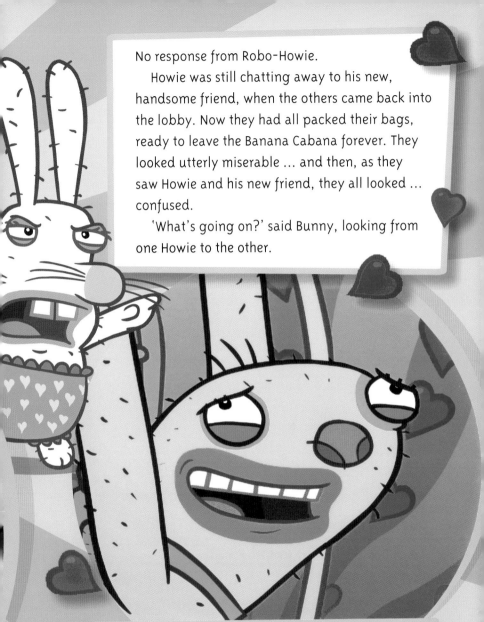

'Two Howies?' whispered Sloth. 'Two Howies! It's like a dream come true!'

'Two Howies,' said Howie, turning to his super-good-looking friend. 'Wait. That's where I recognise you from. You're ... ME!'

'Two Howies,' said Octo, sounding worried. 'Wait ... That means one of them must be a fake!'

'And the FAKE Howie must be the one who tried to fire us!' said Bunny. 'Oh, he is IN FOR IT!'

<u>Something you should know</u>
<u>about Bunny</u>:
When Bunny gets angry,
she gets REALLY angry.
She's got a serious kick.
Her paws can do some damage.
You do not want to cross this rabbit.

Batty was quaking inside the robot. This plan was really not going quite to plan.

'He's the fake!' Batty shouted from inside the robot.

'What?' said Howie. 'You're not Howie!' said Howie.

'You're not Howie,' said Robo-Howie.

'You're not Howie,' said Howie.

'You're not Howie,' said Robo-Howie.

'No, you're not Howie!' said Howie.

'No, you're not Howie,' said Robo-Howie.

'Somebody stop this!' said Octo.

'What are we going to do?' said Octo. 'How will we ever tell who the real Howie is?'

Sloth, on the other hand, wasn't too worried about the dilemma. *Two Howies,* she thought. *Two Howies means ... Two weddings. Two honeymoons. Two dates to see my favourite movie. Two romantic dinners each evening. Two long walks along the beach ...*

Double Howie.

Double everything!

All Sloth's dreams were coming true.

'Is it too late to suggest that we keep them both?' she asked.

'I know how we can tell who the real Howie is,' said Bunny, who'd just had a brainwave. 'And when we find out which one of you tried to kick us all out of the hotel, I'm going to teach him a lesson he'll never forget!'

She poked both the Howies, and they knew she meant business.

'So. Let's find out, right NOW.'

The Howies both gulped. She really was one formidable rabbit.

CHAPTER 5

'Are the Howies ready?' yelled Bunny. Both Howies were standing on the rickety wooden platform outside the Banana Cabana. Inside Robo-Howie, Batty was shaking.

'Both Howies will now perform the triple, quadruple, tightrope, quasi-vertical flight of fear!' Bunny announced. 'And when they get to the end, we'll find out who the real Howie is!'

What? thought Batty. *The triple, quadruple, vertical flight of ... what?!*

But Batty didn't have time to think, because Bunny waved her green flag.

'GO!' shouted Bunny.

They were OFF!

They both dived off the start board, and flew down the wooden ramp ...

They both shimmied along the tightrope of impossibility....

They sprang on to the springboard of terror...

Robo-Howie dived into the giant three-storey super-fast spiral slide.

And then Howie went smack into it.

He landed on it, with his face.

'OOOOOWW!' yelled Howie.

Inside the giant three-storey super-fast spiral slide, Batty had his hands over his eyes. He was a bat! A simple bat! He wasn't used to high speeds. Now he really *really* wished he had gone to clown college. This was it. This was not going to end well. It couldn't, could it?

The inside of Batty's mind was a jumbled, worried place.

Batty's thoughts:
This is not good.
Bubblegum.
Think of bubblegum.
That's better.
Wait. No! I'm still on the ride!
Help!
HELPP!!
HELLLPPPP!!!

The robot whizzed around all the bends, clattered down the slide, and came whooshing out of the bottom, neatly running over the real Howie, who was lying, flat out, on the ground.

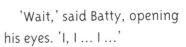

'Wait,' said Batty, opening his eyes. 'I, I ... I ...'

51

'I did it. I DID IT!' said Batty.

Robo-Howie jumped up and down in front of the crowd. For once, Poodle wouldn't be angry with him! For once, he hadn't messed something up! Maybe, for the first time in his life, Poodle would reward him, by letting him have some bubble gum!

'I DID IT!' Robo-Howie shouted.

'I did it!' Batty yelped down his walkie talkie to Poodle.

'You did it!' Poodle shouted back. 'We did it! Or rather, I did it! Now Howie's old friends are going to kick him out forever!' She giggled. 'Wait ... you were INSIDE THE ROBOT? Oh, never mind. The point is that I WIN!'

Poodle licked her lips.

Finally, the Banana Cabana was so close to being in her hands! Finally, she would have the hotel she had always dreamed of ...

'Yes, you did it,' said Bunny. 'Congratulations, Howie!'

Bunny shook Robo-Howie's hand. Vigorously. There was a glint in her eye that Batty didn't like.

'Unfortunately for the fake Howie, he failed to realise that the real Howie can't, no matter how hard he tries, complete the triple, quadruple, tightrope, quasi-vertical flight of fear. Which means that this Howie is ... the fake. Get him!'

'Uh-oh!' said Batty, with a gulp.

It seemed like a good time to run.

Batty burst out of the robot's back door. He started running away, on his tiny little legs.

'Batty?!' shouted Bunny. 'What are you doing? Is this one of Poodle's plans? Oooh, I knew she would be behind this. Oooh, when I get you …'

Batty ran as fast as his tiny legs would carry him. He ran all the way up the enormous metal slide …

He ran round bend after bend after bend, right to the very top.

Phew! thought Batty. *I'm escaping!* … just as he shot out of the top of the slide, and fell through the air, landing at the bottom of the slide, on his head.

'OW,' Batty groaned.

'Batty?' came a voice from his walkie-talkie. 'Batty! When I get my hands on you ...'

Uh oh, Batty thought.

CHAPTER 6

'Sorry for not believing you,' Octo said to Howie, as they trooped back towards the hotel.

'Sorry,' said Piggy.

'Sorry,' said Sloth.

'Sorry,' said Narwhal.

'Car parts,' said Duck.

'That's OK,' said Howie, dusting himself off. He was actually feeling pretty pleased with himself. The tiny stars were dancing in front of his eyes again.

'You know I could have landed the triple, quadruple, tightrope, quasi-vertical flight of fear if I wanted to, right?'

'Sure you could, sure you could,' Bunny reassured him.

'In fact, maybe I'll try again. Starting tomorrow.'

'Oh, Howie,' said Octo, softly.

'I know just what you're going to say, Octo,' said Howie. 'It's OK.' You don't need to say it. Yes, you can come and watch me!'

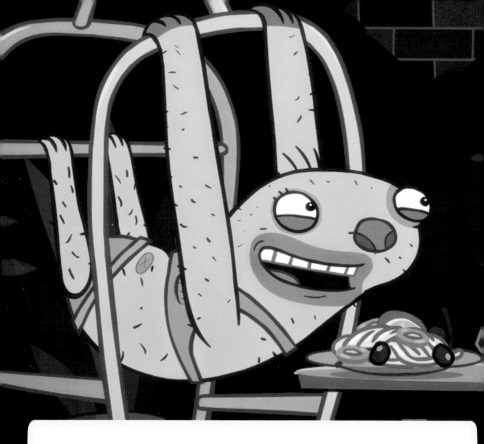

Now, you might think that the broken, abandoned robot had been forgotten about. After all, what would anyone want with a heap of metal that electrocuted anything within reach?

Well.

That night, Sloth was in heaven. She was sitting across the table from the most handsome animal she'd ever dated. The only animal she'd ever dated.

The atmosphere was electric. Probably because of all the sparks that kept exploding out of Robo-Howie's head.

'So, Howie,' she said, 'how are you enjoying your linguine?'

'sdkjslkdjf, ghurgghh, nrghghth,' said the garbled voice of Robo-Howie, which really had seen better days. Unlike Sloth, who had definitely never seen a better day.

This day was THE BEST.

'Oh, Howie, that's priceless,' she said.

'ghghghgh, urgh rghk,' said the robot.

'Howie,' she giggled, 'you're so funny.'

She gazed across the table at him, as clouds of thick black smoke started to rise from his head. The robot fizzed, and sparked, and eventually, with one gigantic spark, its head fell off and landed in the linguine.

'Howie, you're such a charmer!' said Sloth.

It really was the perfect date.

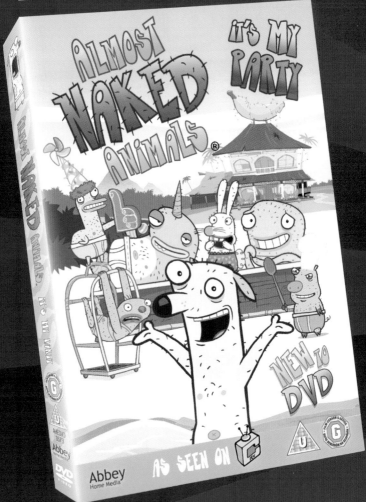